DREAMWORKS
DRAGONS
THE Dragon GAMES

adapted by Tina Gallo

SIMON SPOTLIGHT

New York London Toronto Sydney New Delhi

SIMON SPOTLIGHT
An imprint of Simon & Schuster Children's Publishing Division
1230 Avenue of the Americas, New York, New York 10020
First Simon Spotlight edition May 2015
DreamWorks Dragons ©2015 DreamWorks Animation LLC. All Rights Reserved.
All rights reserved, including the right of reproduction in whole or in part in any form.
SIMON SPOTLIGHT and colophon are registered trademarks of Simon & Schuster, Inc.
For information about special discounts for bulk purchases, please contact Simon & Schuster Special Sales
at 1-866-506-1949 or business@simonandschuster.com.
Manufactured in the United States of America 0415 LAK
1 2 3 4 5 6 7 8 9 10
ISBN 978-1-4814-3288-7
ISBN 978-1-4814-3289-4 (eBook)

Every year the villagers of Berk came together to test their strength, endurance, and courage in the annual Thawfest games.

Hiccup had never won a Thawfest event. Snotlout, on the other hand, won every year. But this year was different. Because this year, for the first time ever, the Thawfest games included dragons!

The morning before the games, Snotlout came flying into the arena on Hookfang. He did a slide stop right in front of Hiccup and Toothless and blew dirt all over Hiccup. Toothless growled at Hookfang, who snorted back at him.

"You know what I love about the Thawfest games?" Snotlout asked. "Winning!" He gave Hiccup a nasty smile.

"My family has never lost a Thawfest," Snotlout said. "Ever!"

"Here we go . . . ," Astrid said, rolling her eyes.

"Dragons or no dragons, I'll do what I do every year. Bring glory to my clan," Snotlout said. Then he turned back to Hiccup. "And you'll do what you do—embarrass yours."

Hiccup didn't say anything. Toothless growled again.

Snotlout laughed as he flew off on Hookfang. "I will crush you all!" he yelled.

Later that night, Chief Stoick walked into Hiccup's room. "What are you two working on?" he asked.

"Just some ideas for Thawfest," Hiccup told him, measuring Toothless' wing.

"Ah, excellent," Stoick answered. But he didn't leave.

"Did you need something, Dad?" Hiccup asked.

"I was just thinking . . . Well, with the dragons, you could actually . . ."

"What? Beat Snotlout? Best the Jorgensons?" Hiccup asked.

Stoick smiled. "When you put it that way, it does have a nice ring."

The opening day of Thawfest dawned bright and sunny.

Stoick was the master of ceremonies. "Let the Thaw Festival games begin!" he shouted. Everyone cheered.

Snotlout's father, Spitelout, grabbed Snotlout by the horns of his helmet and leaned in close to his face.

"What do we say?" Spitelout asked.

"Snotlout, Snotlout! Oy! Oy! Oy!" they shouted together. Then they knocked helmets.

The first event was the sheep lug. At the sound of the bell, the Dragon Riders sprinted from the starting line carrying sheep over their shoulders.

Snotlout burst across the finish line first, snapping the rope. Astrid was second, followed by Tuffnut, Ruffnut, and Fishlegs. Hiccup was last. He dragged himself across the finish line and fell flat on his face, exhausted.

"The first point of the Thawfest games goes to Snotlout!" said Mulch, who was announcing.

"That's my boy!" Snotlout's father shouted.

Snotlout held out his hand for Hiccup to grab. "Here. Let me help you up." But when Hiccup reached for it, Snotlout quickly pulled his hand back. "Oops! Too slow. As usual."

Snotlout walked off, chuckling. Hiccup was furious.

The rest of the day was the same. The log roll, the ax throw—both events went to Snotlout. And Snotlout continued to taunt Hiccup. "That's how it's done, dragon boy," he said.

"Show off," Hiccup grumbled.

Snotlout's dad shouted across the arena to Stoick, "Why don't you just give us the medal now, Stoick? Save your boy the embarrassment."

"Why don't you take a seat, Spitelout?" Stoick answered.

Meanwhile, Hiccup and Astrid stared at the scoreboard.

"Dead last." Hiccup sighed.

Snotlout swaggered over. "Wow. I have all the points *and* the best looking picture? Unfair!"

"Okay, have your fun now," Hiccup said. "Tomorrow, we have the dragon events—and everything changes."

"I can't wait," Snotlout answered. "Because Hookfang and I, it's like boy and dragon have become one. We're like a 'bragon' or a 'droy.' Or . . . Snotfang!"

As Snotlout flew away, Hiccup shouted after him. "Yeah, well, tomorrow you're going to have to deal with Hictooth!"

Astrid and Toothless both stared at Hiccup.

"Hictooth?" Astrid said.

"Yeah, not my snappiest comeback," Hiccup said. He walked over to Toothless, a look of determination on his face.

"You've spiked your last sheep, Snotfang," Hiccup said. "Tomorrow's a new day!"

On the second day of Thawfest, the first event was hurdles.

Fishlegs and Meatlug couldn't do it. "It's okay, girl, this just isn't our event," Fishlegs said soothingly.

Astrid and Stormfly went next. They flew well, but Stormfly's wing clipped the hurdles.

Then it was Snotlout's turn. "You might want to take notes," he said to Hiccup.

But Hookfang couldn't get low enough under the hurdles—Snotlout's head smacked every one.

Finally, it was Hiccup's turn. He turned to Toothless. "Let's show them how it's done, bud," he said.

Hiccup and Toothless made it through the course without a hitch. They even flipped upside down!

"And Hiccup makes a perfect run!" Mulch announced.

Snotlout scowled. Hiccup turned to Astrid. "Did you hear what he said? Perfect! I believe those are my first Thawfest points ever. I just realized something: I like beating Snotlout!"

Fishlegs whispered to Astrid, "Is he gloating?"

"I'm not sure," Astrid answered. "I've never actually seen Hiccup gloat."

Snotlout zipped over to Hiccup. "Don't get too excited." He held up one finger. "You know what this is? The number of wins I need to end this thing."

Hiccup made a circle with his fingers. "You know what this is? The size of your brain. Oh, wait." He made the circle smaller. "That's better."

Astrid looked at Hiccup reproachfully. Hiccup shrugged. "What? He started it. When we were five."

"I hear Snotlout's going to try a new trick he made up for the freestyle called 'The Rings of Deadly Fire,'" Tuffnut said to Ruffnut. "No one's ever tried it before."

"I'm probably going to win just for coming up with this," Snotlout said. "Let's do this. Fire!" he instructed Hookfang.

Hookfang fired, igniting three large rings. But instead of gliding through the rings, he stopped short, clearly spooked. Snotlout went flying off of Hookfang toward the fiery rings, which landed in a heap.

In the next event the riders had to shoot down figures representing their foes and spare figures representing their friends. Hiccup and Toothless got a perfect score, but Hookfang started blasting foes *and* friends. "What are you doing?" Snotlout yelled.

"For the first time in Thawfest history, we have a tie," Mulch announced. "Tomorrow, Hiccup and Snotlout will go head to head in a race to decide the Thawfest champion!"

Snotlout turned to Hiccup. "I can't believe how lucky you are."

"Keep talking, Snotlout," Hiccup said. "And watch your family's winning streak go up in smoke, just like your 'Rings of Deadly Fire.'"

"You know what I always liked about you, Hiccup?" Astrid asked. "You were a gracious loser. Who knew you'd be such a lousy winner?"

Before he could answer, Astrid walked away.

That night Hiccup showed Toothless a new tail fin he built for him. "This is what's going to make the most difference. A fin as thin as paper and even stronger than before. We'll be able to cut and turn better than ever. Snotlout won't have a chance!"

The next day, Hiccup heard Snotlout's dad talk to him as he stretched.

"Son, have you ever heard the story of when I almost lost the Thawfest games?"

Snotlout looked interested. "No, I haven't."

"That's because it never happened," his dad snapped. "No Jorgenson has ever even come close to losing the Thawfest games. Don't you be the first!"

Before the race started, Hiccup held out his hand for Snotlout to shake. "I just wanted to say, have a good race and may the best Viking win."

Snotlout stared at Hiccup's hand. "Oh, the best Viking will win. Don't you worry your scrawny little self about that."

Hiccup glared at Snotlout. "All right, I tried. If that's how you want it."

Mulch yelled into a goat horn. "Vikings and dragons, take your positions!" he shouted. "On your mark, get set . . . and . . . GO!"

Snotlout took an early lead, but Hiccup and Toothless soon caught up with him. Hookfang zoomed above Toothless, throwing the Night Fury off for a second.

"How's that feel?" Snotlout shouted.

Hiccup didn't answer. "Let's see what this new tail fin can really do," he said to himself. He popped the new tail fin open and Toothless' speed immediately increased. Soon Toothless and Hiccup were right next to Snotlout.

"Okay, bud, let's finish this," Hiccup said to Toothless.

Hiccup glanced at Snotlout as he and Toothless were about to kick it into high gear. To his surprise, he saw Snotlout's eyes fill with tears.

"No! I can't lose! I just can't!" he was saying in a panicky voice.

Hiccup realized he'd taken things too far. This race was far more important to Snotlout than it was to him.

What am I doing? Hiccup thought. Then he whispered, "I'm sorry, Dad."

Hiccup opened Toothless' tail fin wide. It caught the wind and sent them into a tailspin. Hiccup and Toothless flew wildly, crashing onto a cliff top.

Snotlout raced past them to the finish line.

"Snotlout is the winner of the Thawfest games!" Mulch announced.

Snotlout's dad was beaming with pride—and relief. "Now that's a Jorgenson!" he shouted.

"You did your family proud," Stoick told Snotlout as he put the medal around his neck. Then he looked over at Hiccup, smiling widely. He was even more proud of his son.

"I know what you did," Astrid said to Hiccup. "You threw the race."

"I have no idea what you're talking about," Hiccup said. "Snotlout was just the better Viking today."

"No, Hiccup," Astrid said. "No one was a better Viking than you today."

Hiccup smiled to himself. He had realized just in time that certain things were more important than winning—like being a good friend. Even if the friend was Snotlout!